Head
Start
Sept - 89

KAY CHORAO

The Child's Story Book

E. P. DUTTON · NEW YORK

The author and the publisher gratefully acknowledge permission to reprint on pages 43–49 "The Lion and the Hare" by Phyllis Savory from *African Fireside Tales,* Part 1, published by Timmins Publishers, 1982.

Library of Congress Cataloging in Publication Data
The child's story book.
Contents: Jack and the beanstalk—The wonderful
teakettle—Hansel and Gretel—[etc.]
1. Fairy tales. [1. Fairy tales. 2. Folklore]
I. Chorao, Kay.
PZ8.C4398 1987 [E] 87-8899
ISBN 0-525-44328-2

Published in the United States by E. P. Dutton,
2 Park Avenue, New York, N.Y. 10016,
a division of NAL Penguin Inc.

Published simultaneously in Canada by
Fitzhenry & Whiteside Limited, Toronto

Editor: Ann Durell   Designer: Riki Levinson
Printed in Hong Kong by South China Printing Co.
First Edition   COBE   10 9 8 7 6 5 4 3 2 1

This book belongs to

_____

This book is dedicated to my brother,
Ron Sproat, who read dozens of storybooks to me,
even when he probably didn't feel like it.

Contents

Jack and the Beanstalk

An English Folktale

A boy named Jack once lived with his mother, who was a poor widow. She always allowed the boy to have his way, so he became quite spoiled and idle.

One day the widow met her son with tears in her eyes. "You have squandered our money, son, so that there is none left, not even for a bit of bread. We must sell the cow or we will starve."

Sadly, Jack took the cow to sell in the village. Along the road he met the butcher.

"Why are you driving that cow away from home?" asked the butcher.

"To sell," replied Jack.

"Ah," said the butcher. "Would you trade the cow for these beautiful beans?"

And from his hat the butcher produced a pile of beans so bright and colorful that Jack could not resist them. The silly boy accepted the offer and ran home with the beans.

Of course, when he showed them to his poor mother, she wept and bitterly flung the beans out the window.

"You foolish boy, what will become of us?" she cried.

They went to bed without any supper.

The next morning Jack noticed something darkening his window. He ran out into the garden, where his mother had scattered the beans.

To his amazement, Jack discovered that the beans had taken root and had sprung into a thick, twining stalk.

"Mother," Jack called, "the beans have grown into a stalk that reaches into the clouds. I am going to climb it!"

The widow begged her son not to go. But Jack always did exactly as he pleased.

He climbed and climbed, higher and higher, until he reached the top.

Looking around, Jack found himself in a strange country, empty except for a great, dark castle.

Jack knocked on the door of the castle.

A woman answered his knock and led Jack into a large kitchen. She kindly gave him food. Then she hid him in the oven.

"Now, don't let my husband see you. He is a giant, and he would gobble you down for his supper."

No sooner had the wife spoken than the floors shook and the air was filled with a thunderous voice.

"Fee fie foe fum, I smell the blood of an Englishman," roared the giant.

Jack shook with fear.

"You only smell the people in the dungeon," said his wife.

The giant paced up and down, but at last he sat down and ate his supper.

Jack peered through a crack in the oven. He watched the giant eat an enormous quantity of food and then roar to his wife, "Bring me the hen."

The wife brought a fine fat hen.

"Lay," said the giant.

And the hen laid three golden eggs.

After a time, the giant grew sleepy. His eyes closed and he fell asleep.

Jack seized the hen and ran as quickly as he could to the beanstalk and climbed down.

He found his mother crying bitterly. But when Jack showed her the hen, she dried her tears and rejoiced.

For many months Jack and his mother lived happily, but Jack kept remembering the giant's castle.

And one day he climbed the beanstalk again.

This time the giant's wife hid Jack in a closet.

"Fee fie foe fum, I smell the blood of an Englishman," roared the giant.

Jack pressed himself to the back of the closet, and the giant thundered by.

"Bring me my bags of money," ordered the giant.

The wife dragged two bags into the room and left them at the feet of the giant, who was warming himself by the fire.

The giant poured out silver coins from one bag and gold coins from the other.

Jack watched him count the money and stack it into gold and silver towers.

The warm fire made the giant sleepy, and he began to snore. Soon the snoring shook the room like pounding surf.

Jack ran from the closet, grabbed the bags, and returned to the beanstalk.

His mother had grown ill with fear when Jack disappeared, but recovered when she saw him.

Again they lived happily. But one day Jack grew restless. He decided to climb the beanstalk one last time.

The giant's wife was reluctant to let Jack in this time, but he persuaded her.

She hid him in a copper pot.

As before, the giant ate a hearty meal. Then he commanded his wife to bring him his golden harp.

"Play," roared the giant.

Instantly the harp played the sweetest music Jack had ever heard. It lulled the giant to sleep.

Carefully Jack crept out of the pot and took the harp.

"Master, master!" cried the harp.

The giant awoke and began to run after Jack.

"Stop, thief!" thundered the giant.

His footsteps were close behind Jack.

Just in time, Jack reached the beanstalk.

When he reached the bottom, he grabbed a hatchet and chopped the beanstalk. *Crash!* The stalk snapped, and the giant fell headlong into the garden.

Of course, that was the end of the giant, and forever after Jack and his mother lived in peace and contentment.

The Wonderful Teakettle

A Japanese Folktale

Long ago an old priest found a teakettle in a little shop. He bought it and hurried home with it under his arm.

When he reached his temple at the top of a hill, he called to his three pupils, "Come see my beautiful teakettle."

The three boys looked, but all they saw was an ordinary old brass kettle.

While the boys returned to their studies, the priest sat in the next room admiring his new prize. He sat and looked so long that he became sleepy.

Growing restless, the boys peeked in and noticed their teacher fast asleep. As boys will, they began to joke and tumble about.

Suddenly they heard a noise.

"It must be the priest," said one boy.

"Now we will have to behave," said another.

The third was more daring. He crept to the screen and looked into the priest's room.

There he saw the new teakettle spring into the air, turn a somersault, and come down a furry little badger!

As the boy watched, astonished, the badger danced and capered about the room. It danced on the table and up the side of the screen.

The boy tumbled back behind the screen.

"That goblin will dance on me if I am not careful," he cried.

The other boys did not believe him.

"There is no goblin out there. There is just an old teakettle," they said.

And indeed, when they peeked around the screen, they saw nothing but a yawning priest and his old brass kettle.

The priest rose and went to check on the progress of his pupils. He found the three boys busy reciting their lessons.

"What good boys they are," he said. "Now I will have tea."

He lit his charcoal fire, filled his kettle, and set it over the heat.

Suddenly the kettle leaped into the air, spilling hot water all about.

"I am burning. Hot! Hot!" it cried.

And in a flash the kettle turned into a badger with a sharp nose, a bushy tail, and four little legs.

"A goblin! Help! Help!" cried the priest.

The boys ran in and began to chase the badger around the room. They grabbed sticks and began to beat the little animal, but it quickly turned itself into a kettle again. However, the boys' sticks had cracked it.

"Oh, dear!" The priest sighed. "What shall we do with such a kettle?"

Just then a tinker came by. The priest took the kettle to him.

"Here is an old kettle I found. It needs to be mended, so it is useless to me. You may have it."

The tinker took the kettle and mended it, using great care.

That night the tinker awoke to find the badger looking at him.

"You are a kind man, Mr. Tinker. I am a badger now, but I am also a teakettle and many other wonderful things."

The kindly tinker fed the badger some sugarplums, the badger's favorite food, and promised never to set him over a fire again.

In return, the badger learned to sing and dance on a tight-rope, which brought crowds of people to watch. Of course, many of these people bought wares from the tinker, and so he grew more and more famous and more and more rich as he moved from village to village.

As the years passed, the tinker grew tired, so he built a temple on the top of a hill and retired with his badger. And forever after, the badger had all the sugarplums he could eat.

Hansel and Gretel

by Jakob and Wilhelm Grimm

On the edge of a large forest lived a woodcutter and his family.

When a famine fell on the land, the woodcutter could not provide enough to feed his two children, Hansel and Gretel, or their stepmother.

Late one night the stepmother turned to her husband. "We cannot feed the children and still have enough for ourselves. Tomorrow you must take Hansel and Gretel to the deepest part of the forest and leave them there."

"No, wife," said her husband. "That I could never do. The wild beasts would come and tear them to pieces."

"Then we must all four die of hunger," said the woman.

And she left her husband no peace until he sadly relented and promised to take the children deep into the woods.

Hansel and Gretel were so hungry that they were wide-awake in their beds and heard their stepmother's plan.

Gretel wept, but her brother said, "Don't worry, little Gretel, I will find a way to save us."

And when his father and stepmother had fallen asleep, Hansel crept out of bed and gathered a pocketful of white pebbles that glittered in the moonlight.

At dawn the woman woke the children.

"Get up, you lazy things. You must gather firewood in the forest."

She gave each of the children a bit of bread, and the four of them set out on a long walk.

Hansel lagged behind, dropping the white pebbles to mark the path.

"Why do you look back?" demanded the woman.

"To see my white cat on the roof of the house," said Hansel.

"Silly little goose. That is the sun shining on the white chimney. Now come along," she snapped.

When they reached the middle of the forest, the children gathered wood and the woman made it into a bonfire.

"Now lie down and rest, children. We will go into the forest to cut wood, and return for you later."

The woodcutter and his wife disappeared into the forest, and Hansel and Gretel stayed behind. They ate their bits of bread when the sun was high, but when it grew dark and cold, Gretel began to cry.

"Don't cry, Gretel. Look!"

Hansel pointed to a path of white pebbles shining in the moonlight.

They followed the pebbles back to their cottage and fell into their father's arms. He rejoiced at seeing them and promised himself never to harm them again.

But not long after that there was more famine.

"The shelves are bare. There is only half a loaf of bread to eat. We must lead the children deeper into the woods this time, so they can't find their way back," said the stepmother.

The father pleaded. "No. It is best to share our last bit of bread with our children," he said.

But his wife would not hear of it.

Hansel heard and tried to go out for pebbles, but the woman had locked the door.

Early in the morning, the woman roused the children as before and gave them each a tiny bit of bread.

On the walk into the forest, Hansel crumbled the bread and left a trail of crumbs.

This time the woodcutter and his wife led the children deep, deep into the forest, and again they left them sitting alone before a fire. Gretel shared her bread with Hansel, and together they waited until the forest grew dark, so they could see their path of crumbs.

But this time when the moon rose in the sky, there was no path to be seen. The birds had eaten all the crumbs.

The children wandered back through the trees, trying to find their way, but they grew more and more lost.

Tired and hungry, they lay down and fell asleep under a tree.

On the third day of wandering through the forest, the children came upon a beautiful snow-white bird. It sang sweetly and then flew off. Faint from hunger, the children followed the bird, which came to rest on a cottage made of gingerbread.

Joyfully, Hansel and Gretel began to break off bits of the cottage and eat.

> Nibble, nibble, little mouse,
>
> Who is nibbling at my house?

called a voice.

The children answered,

> The wind, the wind,
>
> The child of heaven.

and continued eating.

Suddenly the door flew open and an old woman hobbled out.

"Well, dear children, what has brought you here?" she asked.

Hansel and Gretel told their tale, and the old woman took them into her cottage.

She fed the children and let them tumble, exhausted, into two little white beds.

But when they awoke, they saw that she was not a kindly old woman, but a witch! Her eyes were red, and her sense of smell was as keen as an animal's, and she had an appetite for little children.

She threw Hansel into a cage. Then she shook Gretel and said, "Get up, you lazy thing, and cook something good for your brother. When he is nice and fat, I will eat him."

Gretel began to cry, but she had to do as she was told.

Every morning the witch ordered Hansel to hold his finger through the cage so she could see how fat he was growing.

Hansel knew that the witch had bad sight, so he held out an old bone. Day after day, week after week, Hansel did this, fooling the old witch into thinking that he was still bone-thin.

At last the witch grew impatient. "I will eat him tomorrow, fat or thin," she said.

The next day the witch set a large kettle of water boiling for Hansel, and she lit a fire in her oven.

"Now, creep in and see if the oven is hot enough to bake the bread," said the witch to Gretel.

"Show me how to get in," said Gretel.

"Stupid goose, watch," said the witch. She climbed up and put her head in the oven.

Quickly Gretel gave her a push and slammed the oven door behind the howling old creature.

"The witch is dead!" cried Gretel, running to her brother.

They danced for joy and ran about stuffing their pockets with the pearls and precious stones that filled every corner of the cottage.

"Let us go home now," said Hansel.

And so they set out through the forest, coming at last to a lake. A kind duck took them across the lake, one at a time.

The woods on the far side were well known to them. They hurried to their father's house and rushed inside.

Their father was overjoyed to see them. He had not had one happy hour since leaving them in the forest. The step-mother had died, so the father and his children lived happily ever after.

The Lion and the Hare

A Botswana Folktale

It is said by the people of the Bamangwato tribe that long ago Tau the lion walked through the land until he met a hare named Mmutla.

"It is a lonely business walking all alone," said the hare. "May I join you?"

The lion grunted, but thought it beneath him to answer the hare.

"If I come with you, I will cook and run errands for you," said the hare.

"Very well," agreed Tau. "I will provide the food and you will cook and attend to the housework."

Satisfied, the two returned to the lion's home in a tangle of bushes.

Mmutla looked around in disgust.

"How can you live in such a place? Tomorrow we must build a proper hut."

Tau agreed. And so for several days the two animals gathered young trees, called saplings. These they pushed into the ground and bent the branches overhead to form a roof. Next they wove long grass back and forth, in and out of the branches. And finally they used a long wood needle to bind the grass with twine.

"Uncle, I am hungry," grumbled the hare. "Let us stop working and eat."

"No," refused the lion. "You are the servant. I am the master. We will eat when the work is finished."

The lion was on top of the hut, so the hare pushed the thatching needle up through the grass to him. When the lion pushed the needle back down, the hare looped the twine over Tau's paw, binding it firmly to the roof.

The lion roared in pain, but the hare laughed.

"Our dinner is cooked to a turn," teased Mmutla. And with that he gobbled down the entire dinner.

The lion roared and struggled to free himself. When he succeeded, he started after the hare.

Mmutla leaped down a hole, but not quite fast enough. Tau caught one of his legs.

The hare held a root inside the hole, so the lion couldn't pull him out. "You will never catch me that way, uncle," he shouted. "You are pulling on a root, not my leg."

Believing the sly hare, Tau dropped the leg.

"Uncle, it was kind of you to let me go like that," teased the hare from inside the hole.

Tau waited for Mmutla to come out of his hiding place, and when he did, the lion chased him until they came to a wide river.

With a pounce, Tau caught his sly friend.

"O Mighty One," sobbed the hare. "Do what you like with me. Eat me. But please do not throw me across the river. I have enemies there. Anything but that!"

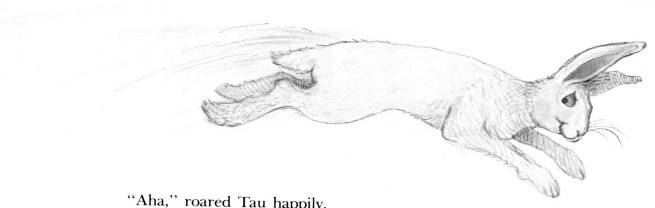

"Aha," roared Tau happily.

And with that he hurled the hare across the river.

Mmutla landed gracefully on the other side and ran away laughing.

However, Tau, seeing that he had been tricked again, climbed onto a log and floated across the river.

"This time I will EAT you," roared the lion.

The hare looked around him in despair. How would he escape this time? His mischief had led him into a difficult spot. But just then he noticed a swarm of bees in a nearby tree.

"I admit, my good uncle, that you are right to be angry, but do not forget that it is customary to give thanks before you eat."

The lion obediently closed his eyes, and the hare quickly hurled a stone at the bees. They swarmed down and bit the lion while Mmutla disappeared into the long grass.

"No matter how long I have to wait, I will catch that rascally hare," fumed Tau.

Weeks later his chance came.

Mmutla was sleeping at the foot of a cliff, under an overhanging rock.

The lion crept up and caught the sleeping hare.

The hare cried, "The rock is falling. Help hold it, good uncle, or we will both be crushed!"

The slow-witted Tau raised his paws to hold the rock.

Quick as a flash Mmutla ran away, and Tau never caught him again.

The Pied Piper

by Joseph Jacobs

In a sleepy little town of long ago, there was a terrible problem. Rats. The problem was rats. They lived in closets, bedrooms, storerooms, upstairs and down, all over town. They scurried, hurried, squeaked, and shrieked.

Even the cats had been driven away by the wild, ugly rats.

The mayor tried poison, rattraps, rat catchers, and everything he could think of, but nothing could rid the town of its terrible problem.

Then one day a strange fellow arrived, dressed in a rainbow of colors. He was tall and thin and had strange little eyes, and he played a pipe.

"I can rid your village of every single rat, but you must pay me what I ask," said the piper.

"Anything," said the mayor.

"Yes, anything," said all the villagers.

"Then we will make it one hundred pounds," said the piper.

"Agreed," said the mayor.

"Yes, agreed," said the villagers.

And so the piper played his pipe up one street and down the next, passing through every corner of the village.

The rats tumbled out of cracks, out of windows, out of doors, and from every hiding place imaginable.

The piper led the squealing parade of rats to the edge of the river. He stepped into a boat and continued to play his pipe while he drifted into deep water.

The rats followed him because, of course, rats swim, but when the tide flowed out, the rats sank into the river mud.

When the tide flowed back in, the piper returned to shore, and the rats were swept out to sea by the fast flowing water.

The piper returned to the mayor for his payment.

The mayor and the villagers shook their heads. The town money chest was almost empty. One hundred pounds seemed to them far too much money for such a simple act.

"Come now, people. A bargain is a bargain," said the piper.

"Would you threaten us?" yelled the mayor.

"Very well," said the piper. "I know other tunes on my pipe. And these may not please you so well."

The mayor and the villagers laughed at the piper and turned their backs.

So the piper began to play. The tune was joyful, full of
laughter and merry play.

And as he paced the streets, children began to follow him.
At first just a few followed, but soon there were dozens, then
hundreds of children, big and small. They danced and joined

hands and laughed and followed the piper right out of the village.

The elders stood stunned with surprise and then terrible fear as the laughter of their children faded forever into the distant hills.

The Ugly Duckling

by Hans Christian Andersen

Near the walls of an old castle, a duck had built her nest. She sat a long time, and finally the eggs began to crack.

"Peep, peep," piped the baby ducklings, poking their heads out of their shells.

Soon all the eggs but one had broken open, and all the ducklings were wobbling around on their little legs.

"How big the world is," they said.

The duck looked proudly at her young. "Do you think this is the whole world?" she said. "That stretches all the way to the pastor's wheat fields."

She counted her ducklings and noticed that one egg had not hatched.

"I must sit on my last and largest egg before we explore the world." She sighed.

An old duck waddled up. "That may be a turkey egg," she said. "I was once fooled in that way. He was a great deal of trouble because he was afraid of the water."

The mother duck said nothing. She sat patiently on the egg until it began to crack.

Out of the shell stepped a big, ugly, gray bird.

The duck looked at it in surprise.

"He's very big for his age," she said.

Next day the sun shone and the mother duck led her babies into the water for their first swim.

Splash! All the ducklings floated beautifully, even the big, ugly, gray one.

"No, he's not a turkey," the mother duck said. "He uses his legs well and holds his neck very straight."

She led her young into the barnyard.

"Now, stay near so that no one steps on you. Beware of the cat," she warned. "And don't turn your toes in."

The ducklings did as they were told, but the other ducks said, "Look at that one duckling. How ugly he is."

One duck flew at him and bit his neck.

"Let him alone," quacked the mother duck.

But day after day all the barnyard fowl chased and teased and bit the poor duckling.

At last he ran away.

"I am so ugly, I must never go back to the barnyard," he said.

He made his way to a wide marsh, where he spent the night.

In the morning a flock of wild ducks flew up from their resting place.

"You are an ugly duckling, but you may live here if you like," they said.

Then out of the sky flapped two wild geese.

"You're so ugly I like you," said one of them.

But shots rang out and the geese fell into the water, killed by some hunters.

A hunter's dog stopped, looked at the ugly duckling, and then went on.

"I am so ugly the dog does not even want to bite me," said the duckling.

He left the marsh and found a hut where an old woman lived with her cat and hen. There the duckling stayed for some days. But he was not happy. He longed for water to swim in.

So he left the hut. He found a lake where he could swim and dive. But he was left all alone.

Autumn came. Once, he saw a flock of dazzling white swans rise into the air, spread their long wings, and fly away to the south. The ugly duckling stretched his neck and made such a strange, loud cry that he frightened even himself.

Cold weather came and the water froze. The duckling barely lived through the long, hard winter.

But one day the sun was warm again. It was spring. He discovered that he could spread his wings and fly.

He flew over a beautiful garden with a winding canal. Three lovely swans floated lightly on the water.

The ugly duckling flew into the water and swam toward the swans. They ruffled their feathers and came toward him.

Fearing they would hurt him, the ugly duckling bowed his head. But when he looked into the water, he saw that he was not an ugly duckling but a beautiful swan.

The other swans swam round and round him.

And from the shore a child cried, "Look, there is a new one! The most beautiful swan of all!"